The Walkie talkies

Hawys Morgan

Illustrated by Lisa Molloy

Schofield & Sims

Zane and Tyler were twins. It was their birthday on Sunday.

They planned a party at the busy swimming pool where their mother worked.

I can't wait for Sunday!

The day before the party, Zane and Tyler whirled around the kitchen while their cake baked.

They laughed and twirled down the hall.
Then the worst thing happened.

Zane slipped on the floor and fell over. His leg was sore.

Then it was time for Tyler and the others to search for gold coins.

Zane was sad that he couldn't search with them.

Tyler gave Zane the map and one of the walkie-talkies.

Tyler took the other walkie-talkie. He heard Zane tell him where to search.

The children found all the gold coins and gave some to Zane.

Thanks to the walkie-talkies, Zane and Tyler had the best birthday!